MATTHEW AND MIDNIGHT PILOT

by Allen Morgan
Illustrated by Michael Martchenko

Stoddart Kids

Published in Canada in 1997 by
Stoddart Kids,
a division of Stoddart Publishing Co. Limited
34 Lesmill Road
Toronto, Canada M3B 2T6
Tel (416) 445-3333 Fax (416) 445-5967
E-mail Customer.Service@ccmailgw.genpub.com

Published in the United States in 1997 by
Stoddart Kids
a division of Stoddart Publishing Co. Limited
180 Varick Street, 9th Floor
New York, New York 14207
Toll free 1-800-805-1083
E-mail gdsinc@genpub.com

Distributed in Canada by
General Distribution Services
30 Lesmill Road
Toronto, Canada M3B 2T6
Tel (416) 445-3333 Fax (416) 445-5967
E-mail Customer.Service@ccmailgw.genpub.com

Distributed in the United States by
General Distribution Services
85 River Rock Drive, Suite 202
Buffalo, New York 14207
Toll free 1-800-805-1083
E-mail gdsinc@genpub.com

Reprinted in September 1999

Canadian Cataloguing in Publication Data

Morgan, Allen, 1946–
Matthew and the midnight pilot

ISBN 0-7737-5852-6

I. Martchenko, Michael.   II. Title.

PS8576.0642M275 1997   JC813'.54   C96-990104-6
PZ7.M67Mat 1997

THE CANADA COUNCIL | LE CONSEIL DES ARTS
FOR THE ARTS | DU CANADA
SINCE 1957 | DEPUIS 1957

*We acknowledge for their financial support of our publishing
program the Canada Council, the Ontario Arts Council, and
the Government of Canada through the Book Publishing
Industry Development Program (BPIDP).*

Printed and bound in Hong Kong, China by
Book Art Inc., Toronto

To Thomas
— M.M.

One evening after supper, Matthew put on his pilot goggles and went out to play with his new glider plane. He tested the wind, then he snapped in the wings, and drew back the band on his sling-shot launcher. He closed one eye so his aim would be true, and let the glider fly.

"Pilot to tower, clear the runway, we're coming in!" Matthew called.

The landing didn't go too well. The glider missed the airport completely and ended up high in a tree.

"Tower to pilot, tower to pilot. It's time to come in and get ready for bed," Matthew's mother called from the porch.

"But my glider's caught," Matthew explained.

"It'll come down eventually," his mother said, as they went inside.

Just before he got into bed, Matthew felt hungry. He looked around in his secret hideout under the bed until he found some candy hearts, an old popcorn ball, and most of a taffy apple.

"Matthew Holmes! What are you doing?" his mother said when she came in.

They talked for a while about food in bed, and in the end Matthew had to admit that his hands were so sticky they'd stick to the sheets. He went to the washroom to wash them clean, and he brushed his teeth again, too. When he returned, his mother was looking out the window.

"I hope the courier comes tonight and delivers my files," she sighed. "I have some work to do this weekend."

"Maybe they got stuck somewhere, just like my glider," Matthew suggested.

"The wind will blow your glider down," his mother told him.

"What if it isn't windy tonight?" Matthew asked.

"Don't worry," she said. "The wind is coming."

She kissed him goodnight and turned off the light. Matthew closed his eyes and listened for the wind.

Around about midnight, Matthew woke up. He heard the sound of the wind outside blowing through the branches. He got up to have a look. He saw that his plane was still in the tree, but it wasn't the only one. Another glider was stuck there too. This one was regular size.

Thump!

Something was up on the roof.

Matthew stuck his head out and looked. A man was standing there. "Is that your plane?" Matthew asked.

The midnight pilot gave a nod. "The wind is tricky tonight," he said. "It blew my glider into your tree. I need to get it free."

Matthew said he'd be glad to help, so the midnight pilot gave him a hand climbing out his window.

"I don't think my mother would like it too much if I walked around on the roof," Matthew told him.

"No need to break your mother's rules. I'll do the work up here myself. You can help from inside the plane."

The midnight pilot snapped Matthew onto a zip line that ran from the house to the tree. Then he gave him a friendly push off the roof and Matthew slid down into the cockpit.

"Grab onto the tree and don't let go till you hear from me," the midnight pilot called. He scrambled up to the peak of the roof and hooked the thick rubber launching band onto the chimney. Matthew held on with all his might as the rubber band stretched tight. The midnight pilot reached out and plucked it.

"Perfect!" he said when he heard the sound. Then he clipped himself to the zip line and slid down into the front cockpit seat.

"OK, let go!" he shouted back.

Twang!

The glider shot right over Matthew's roof. Higher and higher it climbed in the sky until Matthew's house and the entire city were left far below.

"Where are we going?" Matthew asked.

"The midnight air show is on tonight. Everyone will be there."

"Tower to pilot, Courier One, come in Number One," the radio crackled.

The midnight pilot answered the call. "This is Courier One, I read you clear."

"Roger, One. You have a package, downtown hook, level thirty-two."

"Roger and out. We'll make the pick-up as soon as the air show is over."

Before very long they were joined in the air by various other planes. A squadron of dangerous pigeons arrived in their bomber jets. Some grimly determined daredevil ducks came flying in too, sitting backwards with blindfolds on. High overhead, the mysterious moose unfurled a banner and dipped one wing in the secret flyers' salute. A cannon boomed in the distance.

The midnight pilot smiled. "Time for the show to begin," he said. "Let's go."

He peeled away and the others followed. As they approached the air show field, Matthew could see a fleet of tow trucks parked in two long lines. They flicked on their headlights to light up the runway.

As all the air show planes flew past, the crowd below released balloons. Each had a basket underneath full of popcorn balls and cinnamon hearts. The pilots ate as much as they could while they flew their planes over the field in lazy loop the loops.

"Care for a taffy apple?" asked the midnight pilot.

After the air show, the midnight pilot flew straight downtown. The buildings were high and the wind was strong. The streets were like canyons, deep and long.

"Gotta keep both hands on the stick," the midnight pilot called back to Matthew. "You'll have to make the pick-up for me."

The midnight pilot flew in close and Matthew made the grab. His hands were still sticky from all the food, so the package stuck like glue.

"Where's it going?" asked the midnight pilot.

When Matthew looked, he was very surprised. He recognized the address right away.

"It's for my Mom!" he said.

The midnight pilot flew the glider back to his secret hideout.

"It's close to your house, in an underground place that nobody knows but a few of us aces," he told Matthew. "Pull that lever. We're going in."

Matthew tugged on a small, black lever and the wings snapped back to the sides of the plane. They plunged straight down in a nose-first dive. Just when it looked like they'd never survive, they swooped inside a subway tunnel. They zoomed around bends and roared through stations at speeds that defied the imagination.

"Here's our turn," said the midnight pilot. He banked sharply and the glider entered an old, abandoned tunnel.

The tunnel ended at the secret cave. Matthew tugged on the lever again. The wings snapped out and the glider made a perfect landing.

The place was amazing. The walls were made of glassy rock that sparkled like silver. Roots from a tree that grew above ground hung down from the cave's high ceiling.

The midnight pilot hung the glider on one of the roots. Then he led the way up some stairs that spiralled through the trunk of the tree. When Matthew opened the door at the top, he found himself on a branch high above his own front yard.

The midnight pilot threw a zip line across to Matthew's window. As Matthew slid past where his glider was stuck, he reached out and knocked it to the ground. Then he tossed down his mother's package. It landed on the porch with a satisfying thump and Matthew was sure she would find it there. When he arrived in his bedroom again, he waved back triumphantly.

"I got my glider out of the tree! I knew I'd do it eventually."

"A guy needs a plane if he wants to fly," the midnight pilot agreed. "I'm glad you came along tonight. Be my co-pilot anytime. Just let me know when you're free." He waved goodbye and disappeared through the door in the tree.

Matthew climbed into bed and closed his eyes. Soon he was fast asleep.

It was very late, almost quarter to eight, when Matthew woke up the next day.

"Time to get up," his mother told him, as she shook his foot.

Matthew ran to the window. "My plane!" he exclaimed. "It's there in the garden!"

"I knew the wind would blow it down," his mother said.

Matthew laughed and got dressed in a flash, then he dashed straight down to the yard. His mother followed a little more slowly. When she arrived, she was pleasantly surprised. Her package was there just outside the front door.

"It came after all," she said, happily. "I thought they'd forgotten to bring it last night."

"No way," Matthew told her. "We gave that package a very special delivery."

His mother didn't quite understand, so Matthew tried to explain about the midnight pilot and the radio call for Courier One.

"Oh," said his mother. "I think I see." But she didn't really, not at all.

"The midnight pilot's a very nice guy," Matthew told her. "He said I could help any night that I want. You can come too. You'll need to have some sticky stuff to put on your hands. We can buy it at the candy store. And I'll lend you my goggles so the wind doesn't get in your eyes when you jump off the roof."

"Jump off the roof?" his mother echoed.

"Maybe you better have your coffee first, before we get ready," Matthew decided.

"Now you're talking," his mother agreed. "The coffee part I understand."